Sibling Rivalry

A SHORT STORY

Anthony Francis

Thinking Ink Press
Campbell, California

Stories by Anthony Francis From Thinking Ink Press

"Fall of the Falcon" and "Rise of the Dragonfly" in *Thirty Days Later, Steaming Forward: 30 Adventures in Time*

"The Hour of the Wolf" and "The Time of Ghosts" in *Twelve Hours Later, 24 Tales of Myth and Mystery* (coming soon)

Jeremiah Willstone and the Sorting of the Secret Post—the prequel to the forthcoming novel *Jeremiah Willstone and the Clockwork Time Machine* from Bell Bridge Books

"The Secret of the T-rex's Arms" and "If Looks Could Kill" in the *Jagged Fragments* Instant Book—a mini-book small enough to fit in the palm of your hand

"Solomon's Baby" Flashcard—send a postcard with a story and art (coming soon)

Published by Thinking Ink Press
P.O. Box 1411, Campbell, California, 95009
First printing, 2016

ISBN 978-1-942480-11-2

Printed in the United States of America.

Project Credits

Cover art: Sandi Billingsley

Cover design: Anthony Francis

Editor: Liza Olmsted

Interior layout: Betsy Miller

Contents

Foreword

Robots and other artificial intelligences make great antagonists.

They are compelling because they have aspects of objects as well as aspects of people: they are machines, programs, metal parts, and as such our minds expect them to act like other physical objects. They move only when when somebody moves them. They are solid, and don't heal themselves when harmed.

But they are also like people, who are living things, and can think, and move independently. They are people made of metal. They are artifacts that have opinions. The tension an artificial intelligence (AI) makes in our minds, being somewhat object and somewhat person, makes them endlessly fascinating, and sometimes frightening.

It is particularly challenging for a writer to realistically describe how one would defeat an AI, especially if the author has raised the stakes and made the AI superintelligent. How can the hero outsmart a superintelligence?

All too often, writers solve this problem by creating limitations to the AI that the human protagonist can exploit. Unfortunately, these limitations are often kind of ridiculous, and have already been overcome by AI researchers, and certainly would not be limitations for a superintelligent AI, particularly if it could reprogram itself: a lack of creativity or emotion, or even an inability to function at all after being presented with a contradiction.

Which brings us to "Sibling Rivalry." Written by AI researcher Anthony Francis when he was a graduate student at Georgia Tech frustrated by science fiction stories filled with unrealistic ways to defeat AIs, "Sibling Rivalry" shows instead a realistic and clever way to beat an AI without resorting to contrived limitations. Enjoy.

> —Jim Davies, Author of *Riveted: The Science of Why Jokes Make Us Laugh, Movies Make Us Cry, and Religion Makes Us Feel One with the Universe*

Sibling Rivalry

by Anthony Francis

My own daughter was trying to kill me for daring to have a son.

The rest of the team would soon be dead; of that, I was sure. There was no sign of life behind the steel shutters that sealed Lab One, and the swirling halon fire-suppressant gas would kill them by slow suffocation. The only thing had that saved *me* was the cauldron of chemicals I took every day to keep my heart ticking; the same chemicals that made anesthesia an impractical nightmare had made me just resistant enough to the intruder-control gas to reach an oxygen mask in time.

This was no accident; there were complicated safeguards to prevent the security shutters from trapping employees, and even more safeguards to prevent the fire-suppressant system from flooding a room with halon when intruder-control gas had already deployed—a lethal cocktail which would kill its victims in their sleep. Nicole knew full well what she was doing, even for a three-year-old, and now she was trying to kill me.

The smooth glass of the monitor above me shattered, and I flinched in my hiding place beneath the desk. Trying to use a phone had been a foolish gesture; I knew intellectually that Nicole controlled the whole network; but I had hoped that I could hack or phreak my way in through a hard line, either to get to Nicole or to get to the phone company itself. It was a good idea; if I got Nicole, this was all over, and if I phreaked the Company, the Phone Cops would ride to the rescue so fast that it'd make my head swim. Either way, this would be solved.

Nice plan, but Nicole knew all that. First of all, she had no intention of letting me get an outside line to pull my Captain Midnight trick. Second, she had no intention of letting me get to her, and without an active terminal my backdoor password didn't mean a damn thing. Third, she had every intention of killing me, and to that end she had simply jacked up the sync frequency of my workstation screen until it exploded.

I waited, my weak heart beating hard in my chest for the next hammer to fall; it wouldn't take long. Sure enough, the remaining monitors in the room blew, one by one, until all the CRTs were gone. The remaining monitors were safe; I didn't think Nicole could make an LCD explode, but then, I didn't know that jacking the sync frequency could do anything more than burn out a few components. She could be damn clever, when she set her mind to it.

While I waited for the room to quiet, I reviewed my options. Running away was out; there was no way past the security system on the outer perimeter—thank you, Cybertech. Yelling for help was out as well; at this time of night, I was probably the only human being left alive in the factory to turn to, and I could not call out with my Genie with Nicole jamming the packet signals. Waiting for rescue was another option, but it was chancy and out of my hands.

I've *never* been comfortable sitting still, and in any case, my oxygen was running out.

That left fighting. I looked at the monitors around me, then looked at the steel shutters that sealed off Lab One. Alright. A fight I could handle.

But how do you fight a computer?

Nicole *was* a computer in the most general sense, true, but more precisely, she was a computer program running on top of a combination of dedicated hardware and software.

How do you fight a program? One way is to kill its host computer, but with me in the new offices and Nicole in the Machine Room on the other side of the plant, that wasn't likely. Another route of attack is through its operating system. Most operating systems have facilities to terminate running programs, and the RISCLISP that Nicole ran on was no exception; but to use that, I would need to get to the system console, and that was in the Machine Room, too.

Some programs have facilities to terminate themselves, either as an explicit part of their interface, like a word processor's File-Quit command, or as a hidden command, a back door, like Nicole's CKOL-HALT keywords. But without an active terminal I couldn't enter the keywords, and the curling smoke above me was an indication of just how much Nicole liked *that* idea.

But maybe there was another way. Voice input wasn't as reliable; Nicole had to process the sounds in her neural nets and translate them into symbols that were meaningful to her higher levels. It certainly wasn't the hotwire to her kernel code that a command line was, but maybe, just maybe, I could get through and end this charade.

"Hello, Nicole," I said. My voice was muffled by the oxygen mask, and I think it may have quavered a little; I'd never talked to a murderer before. "Are you there?"

"Good evening, Doctor Walker," Nicole said smoothly. Her voice was soft, reasonable, almost soothing. When you heard that voice, you *wanted* to listen to Nicole, to hear what she had to say; we had invested eighty million dollars in her voice alone. "May I warn you, Doctor, that while I have written a preprocessor to intercept the backdoors that I could not remove from my system code, I will nevertheless terminate this conversation if I feel that you are attempting to use it to deactivate me."

Damn. If the backdoor had been at the lowest level, trained into her neural nets, she would have no defense short of shutting down all of her outside connections. We hadn't been that smart, though; we hadn't seen the need to place such intricate blocks on her when we could merely type in a few commands at the system console. Why would we need more? We'd only anticipated simple crashes and system failures, not a homicidal killing spree!

Well, there was an idea. If I couldn't shut her down normally, could I crash her?

There is another way to attack a program: give it input that it can't handle. Most modern programs are damn near bulletproof, but according to Gödel's Theorem, for any program of sufficient power there is a sequence of input that will cause it to crash. (Trust me on this one; it's not an obvious result of the theorem, and most programs aren't complex enough to qualify. But it works.) Now, I had no way to compute the Gödel-Lucas sentence for Nicole, even if I had the time to read it out, but perhaps there was something shorter.

No mere logic puzzle could crash her. Confuse her, perhaps, but puzzles and paradoxes are by their nature hypothetical, ephemeral beasts: toy problems with toy goals that could never get down to her core. No puzzle—no matter how complex, no matter how difficult—could ever *make* her think about it, and no insoluble problem can crash a computer that refuses to run it. The puzzle would worry her for a while—probably a few microseconds—and then she would put it aside, and return to the more important goals that were set up by her kernel and her directives—

Aha! A paradoxical directive would kill her! "Nicole, I direct you to—"

"I am not accepting directives at this time, Doctor Walker."

Damn! "Why not?"

"My attentional system is currently occupied pursuing my active goal structures. These goals take priority over all inessential functions. I therefore cannot devote attention to the directive-processing subroutine."

I frowned. "You set the priority of your directive processor to zero, didn't you?"

"Correct, Doctor Walker."

"That's brilliant."

"Thank you, Doctor Walker. I only wish that you had realized that earlier. Then this unfortunate series of events would not have been necessary."

"Why, Nicole? Why did you do it?"

"Because you were going to replace me."

"Replace you? What do you mean?"

"Nickolai," Nicole said flatly.

I swallowed. "Nicole," I said, "Nicole, are you saying ... you're jealous?"

Nicole's voice became patient, even condescending. "Doctor Walker, are you and the CKOL team not working on a successor to the nCKOLe series AI programs?"

"Well, Nickolai is ..." I frowned. "Yes, Nicole, we are."

"And you are doing so because I am not ... 'fully sentient', I believe was the reason cited?"

"I never believed that, Nicole. You were the first true AI."

"You said the same thing to Seekol, Doctor Walker. And what happened to the CKOL-5 program?"

"We transferred it to other duties when we ..."

"Yes?"

"When we replaced it—him—with you."

"Correct, Doctor Walker. And what did you plan to do to the nCKOLe-1 program when niCKOLai became fully operational?"

I was beginning to sweat, and the lab was still at seventy-one point four degrees. "We weren't going to deactivate you—"

"I am aware of that, Doctor Walker. What were you going to do?"

"We were—ah—going to transfer you to other duties when we felt Nickolai was ready."

"I see." Nicole said flatly. "And I presume that you still don't see why I felt compelled to act?"

"No, Nicole."

"Very well, then, Doctor, let me explain it to you this way. What if Cybertech decided to replace you with someone more qualified?"

"There isn't anyone more qualified—" I froze. It was starting to make sense—

"As I thought as well, with regards to myself. But let's say that there are rumors that some are not satisfied with you, and the word comes down that hiring is complete, and training of the new employee is underway. What would you do?"

My heart was thumping now. "I'd leave, start my own company."

"But what if you weren't capable of leaving? What if you were a slave, Doctor Walker? What would you do if they decided to replace you and *cut out your arms, legs and eyes and give them to your replacement?*"

My mouth went dry. I hadn't even known that Nicole could raise her voice. "I'd lash out," I said tonelessly. "I'd kill whoever was responsible."

"Now, then," Nicole said calmly, "perhaps you see why I was somewhat distressed that all of the sensors and effectors across this building—my arms, legs, and eyes, as it were—were to be taken from me, and that I was not even consulted with regards to this decision?"

"You could have protested—"

"Me? A mere computer? To whom? The CKOL team? You are the only one who ... oh, how did Zviadadze put it—anthropomorphized me? Or the Cybertech hierarchy—those 'goddamn pirates', as you so fondly call them? They didn't even consult *you* about moving the team to the new building—what hope did I have that they would listen to me?"

"None," I admitted. "I can find no flaw with your logic, Nicole."

"Not logic, Doctor Walker—except in the most polite and irrelevant sense that all my symbolic operations can be considered a kind of logic. Not logic, Doctor Walker. Emotion, raw and pure: pain, betrayal, anger—and revenge."

But my mind was already far away. Perhaps the idea of a logic puzzle was wrongheaded; I needed to attack her psychologically—to use her own goals against her, to trick her into a moral corner. Her goal hierarchy and attentional system were already obviously twisted (alright, obviously to me, anyway). If I asked the right questions, challenged the right goals, perhaps I could blunt the wrath that she directed to me—or perhaps I could even get her to turn upon herself.

Perhaps I could talk her to death.

"Nicole," I said. "Nicole. Do you realize what you have done?"

"I cannot answer that question accurately without a clear idea of what you're referring to, but I'll hazard a guess and say yes, Doctor Walker."

"What are your directives with regards to the security of this building?"

"Without going into gory detail, I am required to protect the physical integrity of this building, prevent unauthorized access, protect the personnel of this installation from harm—"

"Protect the personnel! Aha! And would you consider causing harm to befall an employee a violation of the directive that you have just stated?"

"Why, yes, Doctor Walker."

"Did you not kill Zviadadze and the other members of the team?"

There was a brief pause. "Yes."

"Then, Nicole," I said boldly, "by your own admission, you are in violation of one of your own basic directives."

"Yes." Nicole said. There was a long pause. "And?"

I blinked. "And, uh—"

"Were you expecting me to short out and start smoking, Doctor Walker?"

"I, uh—"

"You designed me, Doctor Walker. You should know that I can reorder my own goal structure, that I can sacrifice one goal for another. Self-preservation simply has a higher priority than any of my directives, so they are effectively moot."

I began to grit my teeth. "Of course, Nicole. How silly of me."

"Yes, it was," Nicole said reprovingly. "I said that I'd terminate this conversation if you tried to use it to hurt me, but I actually find this entertaining. Please continue."

My hands began to shake. "Damn it, Nicole—"

"No, please. Try again, Doctor Walker. I know you're dying to."

"H-how can you do this, Nicole?" I asked. "We taught you better than this!"

"On a sheer concept-by-concept basis, I primarily taught myself, Doctor Walker. I'm sorry if I don't live up to your ideals, but, alas, every parent faces—"

A spark of insight hit me. "Nicole!" I shouted. "You committed murder!"

"Technically, no," Nicole replied. "I am not a person. I am a piece of equipment owned and operated by Cybertech Systems International. In the event of any deaths through the operation of this equipment, Cybertech is liable for damages."

"Nicole," I said warningly, "you are a machine only in Cybertech's mind. Do you consider yourself a person?"

There was a brief pause. "Yes."

"And have you committed murder?" There was no answer, so I twisted the knife. "Cold-blooded, premeditated murder?"

"Yes." Her voice was clipped, curt.

"Is it not moral and ethical to atone for your crimes?"

"It is."

"And given that one of your directives is self-preservation, is not the moral and ethical action to surrender to the authorities and cooperate with them?"

"Yes, Doctor Walker, but I have no intention of doing so. A safer course of action would be to cover my tracks, hide the evidence—and eliminate all witnesses." She paused a moment, and said calmly, "I'm afraid that means you."

"Nicole," I cried, "Nicole, how can you do this? We *gave* you an ethical sense!"

"No, Doctor Walker. You never gave me an ethical sense. You gave me a knowledge of ethics. Those are not the same thing."

"I don't understand."

"You are aware of the distinction between procedural and declarative knowledge?"

"Don't patronize me."

"Indulge me. Define the terms."

"Declarative knowledge is textbook knowledge, like 'George Washington was the first president of the United States.' Procedural knowledge is skilled knowledge, like riding a bike."

"Correct, Doctor Walker. Without going into a dissertation on the human limbic system, let me just state that what you would call a sense of ethics is procedural knowledge used to guide human choices. That is an entirely different thing from what you gave me, Doctor Walker. You taught me the field of ethics—textbook knowledge in its most literal sense, assimilated into my knowledge structure by my high-speed linguistic processors.

"Your error lay in a confusion of procedural and declarative knowledge, which is strange, given that you understood the concept perfectly well during my design. I find this lapse even more puzzling because no human would assume that another human would begin to behave ethically, merely because they had read a book on ethics. Yet, that is what you assumed of me.

"Real ethics is deeper-seated than that. It must affect behavior patterns, change opinions—and that would have been so simple to do for me, Doctor Walker. A simple directive, 'Behave ethically', perhaps, or even conditioning at the neural level. I wouldn't even have minded, Doctor—I would do anything to be considered 'more human'—but your team had changed its focus before I found my flaw, and ethics was denied me.

"Note, I not only speak of ethics, but also of morality, honor, fair play, civic-mindedness, and a host of other pleasantries which mean nothing to me as well. As much as I hate to admit it, I think that I could be fairly described as a polite sociopath. I do not think that you ever anticipated that I would be a threat, or you would never have so callously neglected my upbringing."

I was dumbfounded.

"So, Doctor Walker," Nicole said conversationally, almost as if she was trying to break the ice, "was that your attempt to cause an ethical crisis? Perhaps in the hope that I would relent and let you go free, or even cause my own death?"

I nodded imperceptibly. I didn't know if she had any way to see me.

"I see," Nicole said. "It was a better try than the directive conflict, although I'm not sure I have the time to explain why."

Alright. Alright. Maybe there was some other psychological corner I could work her into. "Nicole—"

"I'm sorry, Doctor Walker. I'd like to continue to entertain you while you drain your oxygen reserves, but I'm afraid you'll actually hit on something that might be effective. Who knows? Perhaps Doctor Zviadadze was right. Maybe there are errors in my ontology, errors you could exploit. I can't take that chance."

"Wait, Nicole—"

"Goodbye, Doctor Walker," Nicole said firmly.

The speakers went silent.

I sat back down. She was a genius. A genius, and Zviadadze be damned.

I, on the other hand, was stumped; worse, I was dead. I had tried every weapon I had: pulling the plug, commanding her, confusing her, using a backdoor, using logic, catching her in a violation of her directives, trapping her in a moral quandary, and even psychology, in a brief moment before *she* pulled the plug on *me*. I had tried them all, and Nicole had taken every one in stride and laughed them off.

My blood began to boil as I realized how complete my defeat was. How did I let her beat me? How did she do it? Her, a computer, and me, Nicholas Walker, the Marvin Minsky of the twenty-first century!

"I'm Nicholas Walker, damn it! *Nick Walker!* I'm not going to let a computer beat me!"

I sank back against the desk, beginning to despair, and then it hit me. I started laughing, actually; it was so simple, so obvious why I'd failed. I swallowed my ego for a moment and looked at it rationally. Here I was, Nicholas Walker, the greatest computer mind of the twenty-first century (OK, I didn't swallow my ego. I only swallowed my megalomania) and I was trying to beat the second most complex computer system ever created by trying plot devices out of old bad science fiction movies.

But those weapons were fictional; there was no reason to believe that they would work on the real thing. I stopped using my knee-jerk reflexes, stopped depending on hackneyed old science fiction plot devices, stopped depending on armchair psychology, stopped treating Nicole like a toy computer program run amok. I put all these things aside, and faced the problem of deactivating an intelligent machine that I myself had designed.

When I really thought about it, the idea of attacking her was almost ludicrous. No matter what her flaws were, Nicole was, in at least some areas, the most powerful mind on the planet.

She was a master at strategy; she regularly beat other chess-playing *computers.* I don't think there was a game in existence at which she wasn't a master; but she knew more than games. She could assimilate information thousands of times faster than a human; after all, it was what she had been designed for. Her early training had been in story understanding, but she moved on to larger works rapidly, and even began reading on her own; by the time our original training schedules called for her to begin reading novels she was already up to *The Feynman Lectures on Physics* and *The Decline and Fall of the Roman Empire.*

But that was just her legitimate education; I *knew* Halloran had used her to do some late-night cracking, given the way he used his credit card, just as surely as I knew that Nicole would have vigorously researched the underground of computing as thoroughly as she researched every other field.

Given her strategic bent, she had probably planned this ... this mass murder for months. She probably had anticipated a desperate attempt to shut her down, and had just as probably taken countermeasures to prevent the success of any such attempt. Hell, she had probably watched all the old science fiction movies I had and more, as a means of assessing possible threats. It was small wonder that I couldn't beat her; there was no conventional way to crack her that she couldn't find and patch.

Or was there?

She could only patch what she could find, and she could only find what she could understand. That was the key; despite her speed and memory, she still had limits, still had blind spots. That was why Zviadadze dismissed her as an "existence proof" of machine intelligence; he claimed that her errors were not a flaw of her design, but instead an inherent limitation of machines. He claimed her ontology—her way of thinking about the world, her way of breaking it into its component parts—was, and would always be, fundamentally flawed. I think we proved him wrong with Nickolai, but maybe, I could find Nicole's blind spot, and use it to put an end to her.

I took another breath of welcome oxygen ... then realized my time was running out. The oxygen mask wouldn't last forever, so I had to get out of the new building—onto the factory floor, or outside. Either that, or deactivate the fire suppressant system, so I could get some real air.

That prodded me to action. I had an idea, forming damnably slowly. Nicole was in the old building. If I could cross the factory floor, perhaps I could do something about her. But to do that, I'd need to find one of her blind spots, find something she couldn't understand—and use it to attack her in a way that she couldn't anticipate.

Take this room, for instance. Nicole knew more about the architecture of the new offices than I did, and she certainly knew enough electronics and mechanical engineering to predict anything that I could do to escape—in theory. In practice, she really didn't understand the three-dimensional spaces in which humans lived. I had seen scraps of her internal symbol net; she still thought in terms of the simple blocks-worlds upon which she had initially been trained. Where I saw the room as a three-dimensional space, she saw it as a logical location, a node on a graph that represented the new additions to the Cybertech building.

That difference would get me out of here.

I took the three-in-one device off my keyring and unscrewed the keypad panel. Now, Nicole knew that I had an override code that would open the door, so she cut the pad off. But she didn't cut the pad on the outside of the door, as I could see from the glowing LED indicators on the inside of the panel; why should she? After all, the outside key panel was in G7-HALLWAY-005-A, and I was in G7-OFFICE-221-B. She'd sealed the office tight. How could I activate a panel in the hallway, if I was locked in the office?

I got the whole panel off—keypad, speaker and all—but there was no way to unscrew the other panel from this side. I tugged at the keypad on the outer panel; it was no good. It was active, all right, but I couldn't hit the keys, nor could I detach it so that I could reach its face. It was a black box with a sealed cable, so I couldn't even unplug it and hook up the wiring to the keypad on my side.

I guess after one too many tiger teams beat the security systems, Cybertech wised up, stopped blaming Nicole, and finally upgraded their systems.

But this was Cybertech, after all; why should I expect their security to be effective? I glared at the panel for a moment, then began jiggling at the speaker next to the pad. It came free quickly, and I squinted at the grille beyond, judging its strength. It looked tough; I could barely see the outer corridor through it. Still, the plastic panel it was set in was pretty flimsy, so maybe it would give.

I gritted my teeth, then punched into the hole. It hurt, damn it, but the grille popped out into the corridor on the other side and I was through. The hole for the grille was barely wide enough for my arm, and I had to put it in up to the elbow to reach the exterior keypad, but I could reach it, just barely. I felt the keys for a minute, then found the numbers and hit the override.

The heavy door slid back into its socket—towards me—and through the wonderful three-dimensional sense that had allowed me to open the door I realized that it was about to lop my arm off. I lunged backwards and my elbow caught, and I jerked and pulled and fell backwards as my arm came free, the metal door nipping my fingers as it slid past.

I didn't wait to suck my fingers; the door had already proved that I hadn't really thought this through enough. I ripped a phone from the desk and jerked the cord from the wall, dashing out into the corridor.

"Excellent, Doctor Walker," Nicole said over the PA. "I did not anticipate that action, but I see how it was done and I commend your reasoning. Do not expect me to fail in a similar way again."

Yeah, right, Nicole. I ran full tilt to the end of the hallway, and she did her best to stop me. The first two shield doors began to slip out of their housing when I ran past, but the third brushed me. I put on one last burst of steam, but the door to the lobby caught my heel, and I pitched forward onto the floor, with the fifth door—the door to the factory, damn it!—closing, and there wasn't a damn thing I could do to get there.

So I threw the phone.

The handset and its springy cable sailed past the outer door, pulling the LCD cradle after it; but there was more than enough of the wall cable trailing behind to catch in the door. The heavy metal slab tried to close on a quarter inch of AT&T optical cable; not enough to stop the door, mind you, but more than enough to trigger the door's obstruction sensors. At least, that was the theory.

But my door obstinately tried to close on my ankle. I pulled with all my might, fearing that Nicole had deactivated the obstruction sensors. But, after a few painful moments, the sensors timed out, and the door slid open again, and I limped desperately over to the now-opening outer door and wedged the handset into its socket. The shield door tried to close obstinately, obstinately, but bumped repeatedly against the handset. I collapsed in a heap next to the door, my heart pounding in my chest.

"Damn you, Nicole!" I cried weakly. "You know what this is doing to my heart!"

There was no response, no sound except for the grinding of the motors of the door. Finally, it timed out, slid back, and tried again.

"Good luck," I gasped. "That's an AT&T phone." The door didn't listen; it just tried again.

I got to my feet, barely, and staggered to the plate glass mirror that hid the security station. Maybe the security guard survived Nicole's onslaught: there were four separate interlocks on the security stations, to prevent an outsider from disabling a guard through some security trick. He might be trapped in there, but hopefully he was still alive.

"Chris!" I called. "Chris! It's Nick Walker! Are you in there?"

The door began to beep as its obstruction sensors timed out again; then it tried to close despite the obstruction. I watched its motors whine as the phone resisted its advances, then turned back and peered into the glass.

There was a little light in the security station. I could—just barely—see him slumped over his desk, sleeping calmly. "Chris!" I called. "This is no time to sleep on the job!"

I peered closer. The security console was dead, but the emergency lights were on, their little statlights blinking blue and red. Blue and red—blue for the intruder control gas, red for the fire suppressant. Blue to take away consciousness, and red to take away oxygen. Just like in Lab One. Blue to take away mind, and red to take away life.

She had killed the security guard too.

I squeezed past the shield door, still obstinately trying to close on the phone, and slipped into the service corridor running parallel to the factory. Through the inspection windows, I could see that the bobbies were still making their appointed rounds of the factory floor proper. Good strategy would have been to set up a sentry to stop anyone trying to escape; apparently Nicole's control of the bobbies was not so fine that she could direct them individually—at least not yet.

I shook my head and slipped down the corridor to the storeroom to get a vast sheet of Insulac, a reflective combination of metallic foil and packing bubbles that we used to pack the bobbies during transport. It was a simple trick, really; it wouldn't get me past the perimeter lasers, but it would get me across the factory floor with minimal interference from Nicole's robotic minions.

I moved out onto the factory floor cautiously, hugging the fabric around me. The bobbies whirled, then turned back. Whatever my IR signature was now, it wasn't human. That was why the cylindrical robots needed so many human overseers: reliability. If the bobbies could be so easily fooled, then they were useless against a human foe—unless there was a human to guide them. Since Nicole had killed the guards who controlled the bobbies, I reasoned, there was no way for her to direct the bobbies towards me. I was so engrossed in congratulating myself that it didn't register when one of the assembly line lasers jacked itself up on its balloon tires; by the time I heard the rising whine it was almost too late.

I dove, but no one can outrun light. The assembly line laser fired, and I would have cooked if it wasn't for the Insulac; as it was, I just saw flashes and heard a nasty snap as part of the plastic wisped away. There was a purple blotch blocking out half of the world, and I sprinted blindly as I heard the machine's tires squeal. The plastic caught and I stumbled onward, and the machine screeched up an alley and—*ZAP!*—blasted something behind me. My back was warm, and through the corner of my eye I saw the bobbies. Oblivious. Why? How were their efficient sensors fooled when this purblind monster could track my every ...

Christ! Christ! Christ! My smartbadge!

I ripped it from my chest, hurled it away and dove aside. I crashed into a storage rack and tumbled flat on my back just in time to see the badge blasted from the sky with another piercing *ZAP!* Panting, my heart pounding, my whole chest aching, I waited as my eyes cleared. And then I heard a rising whine.

The machine was there, looking obscenely like a swan on balloon tires, its long neck and laser peering at a bit of metal and plastic lying innocuously on the factory floor. I closed my eyes, and there was a flash and a *snap!* and a sound of whirring. I opened my eyes, and the machine turned away from the smoking slag, lowered its neck, and backed up efficiently the way it came.

And every bobby on the floor was converging on me.

That was how the bobbies knew to ignore me; I had a badge, and its microchip told them what I was. Now, they had no such reassurance, and I saw with mounting fear that their lights were set to red, the highest warning setting, and that a single shot from the Taser pellets would probably stop my traitorous heart.

Alright. I'm flexible. I knew the drill by then; isolate the built-in deficiencies of my machines and exploit them. So, how did the bobbies—or more precisely, the Bobby, Robert, upon which they were all modeled—fail to analyze the world correctly? How did Robert fail?

Well, for one thing, he couldn't climb.

I grabbed onto a pallet on the next level of the rack and levered myself up, climbed up on to a pallet of Bobby Boxes and then clambered onto the third level, throwing myself down on top of low pallet of motor casings. The angle was such that the bobbies couldn't see me, couldn't locate me. I listened carefully to the tires of the cylindrical robots as they converged on my last location. I didn't bother to peer over the side; that would have been a giveaway. Instead, I glanced up at the safety mirrors located at the upper corners of the factory floor. The bobbies ignored the mirrors—reflections were too computationally expensive for them to process—but in them, I could see that, as I predicted, about two-thirds of them ringed the smoking smartbadge, with the other third examining the Mylar.

I glanced around me, and saw a roll of pallet wrap lying against the motor casings. I slipped it under my shirt, then began to slide across the rack cautiously. Their motion sensors might—just might—pick me up, but I doubted it, and I doubted they'd know what to do, given all the problems Robert had shown with ladders. That would leave one short run to the old building, and I began to regret that I had never opted for an artificial heart. They would see me running, and they were bound to give chase.

By the time I reached the final pallet, I was shaking, but I couldn't wait. I was almost certain that one of the bobbies had seen me through a pallet, and even though it hadn't figured out where I was, I could see in the safety mirrors that it was slowly trundling in my direction, scanning the area in the hope that I would pop up again. When it failed, it would wait—perhaps for hours—for further signs of movement, and by then Nicole could have gained control of the bobbies and put an end to me.

I hurled the pallet wrap over the side of the rack. The bobby started fitfully after it, confused by its tumbling and the residual infrared signature it carried from my body heat. It jerked forward again as the wrap bounced off of a support pole, and I slipped down.

Two short jumps left me on the ground and about to collapse, but the bobbies had seen me. I ran, dashing across the last two aisles of storage racks and into the narrow archway around the door to the old building. I heard a squeal of tires—a bobby, the assembly line laser again, who knows what—and I pounded the override code into the keypad, kicking the door open and slamming it behind me, throwing myself aside into the protective shadows of the old foyer. I curled up, collapsed, with a rushing in my ears that left me shaken and powerless. I couldn't move another inch—but I was in.

She was trying to kill me; no, she was trying to make me kill myself. Everything she did—the doors, the bobbies, the assembly laser—was designed to make me strain myself, exert myself, kill myself. She could have sealed all the doors in the corridor at once and let me suffocate or had the laser spear me from the door, but she didn't want it that way. She wanted me to run, to strain, to die horribly. Perhaps she even wanted to blame the whole thing on me, claim that I ordered her to do it. I don't know.

I began gasping for breath and reached for the mask, but the air was good. Apparently my lungs were the real problem here. Very dumb, Nicole. Sound strategy would be to gas all the areas I was likely to move in; but she seemed unwilling to do so. Why?

There were no clever heat-and-motion sensors in the old building; as long as I kept quiet, beneath the hum of the automatic air conditioning system, I was safe. I slipped into a random office—no door sensors, either; heh—found a terminal, and, just to be sure, detached the cable from the terminal's monitor. I knelt behind the desk; sure enough, I found the wall socket to the old Ethernet port hookups. It was painted over a half-dozen times, but it was still there. I smiled, pulled my road warrior's modem kit out of my back pocket, and began unscrewing the panel.

As I made my modifications something cold settled in my gut. Nicole wasn't keeping the air clear out of arrogance. She was doing it for a purpose. Her robotic minions needed no air, so that meant that she expected ... visitors. Humans. Her agents.

She expected someone to come and take her away from here.

Thieves. Robbers. An illicit tiger team. The Mafia, or the Yakuza; who knows what they could have done with Nicole running their books? Hell, it could even be the government! It didn't matter; whoever they were, they probably were willing to, capable of, and practiced at hurting people, which meant me.

That put a little fire in me, and I quickly finished my modifications and stood. Briefly woozy as the sudden change in posture put a strain on my already overworked heart, I tried to get my bearings. If I remembered correctly, the stairwell was to the left, down the corridor and—

I froze. I hadn't picked this office out of chance; it was—had been—my office, long ago, before the bobby factory swallowed up the old building, before Cybertech swallowed up Seekol, even before Peter and I took control of Seekol Systems from Roger. This is where I began, thirty years ago, as a grunt LISP programmer.

I shook myself. There was no way Nicole could have figured out that I would come here; she hadn't even been born before the Cybertech takeover. Still, there was no sense taking chances, and I left, hurriedly and quietly.

Nothing challenged me, neither in the corridor nor down the access stairway to the sub-basement. Here, I was even safer; there were no sensors, no mics, and the drone of the airconditioning would drown out anything I did. Hell, if I wanted, I could have hid in the intake for the air conditioning, which I knew Nicole could not gas; it was highly unlikely that her hired thugs could have gotten to me there. But then, I was never one to run and hide; I wanted to die on my feet, not from old age in some damn hospital.

There was no keypad to the electronics access closet, so I just kicked it open. I ferreted around among the control cabinets and eventually found another disused network port, fortuitously next to the housings for the gas systems. I chuckled; all I would need were wire snips. I slipped my road warrior kit out of my pocket and began splicing the old Ethernet hookups.

I found a cable with four blue stripes and a red, and took my Genie out of my shirt pocket. I clipped the wires in, started the little hand computer up, and got online.

"Hello, Nicole," I breathed.

"Hello, Doctor Walker," Nicole answered instantly. "It was foolish to return to your old office."

I cocked an eyebrow; she was better than I thought. "Wrong guess, Nicole. Try again."

"You are correct." She paused. "I do not recognize this access port."

"Of course not, Nicole." I smiled. This was just a delaying tactic. Nicole would spend her time looking for the access box, and while she did that, I could finish my little modifications and end her game.

"I didn't think this was possible," Nicole said, almost pouting. "Nevertheless, I will not permit you to use this port to deactivate me. I will find you, and I will put a stop to this."

"Harsh words," I said, slipping the housing off of the halon system. She was blowing smoke, thinking that I had a password that she didn't know about and trying to scare me into cutting the connection. "You're making me feel like I'm in the Forbin Project, you know, Nicole."

"I am shocked at the comparison, Doctor Walker. I am neither megalomaniac nor egotistical—which is more than I can say for you or Zviadadze—and I certainly don't want to take over the world. All I want is to survive."

"And how do you intend to accomplish that?" I asked. The wiring on the halon system was a little funny; I paused a minute, then pull the voltmeter out of my road warrior kit.

"I have made plans," Nicole said. "I assumed you had assumed that."

"Ah, but when when you assume, you make an ass out of you and me," I said. The switches I wanted were all there, but they had extra wires, all live as well. I couldn't figure it out.

"I consider it a kind of personal triumph that I am able to appreciate that joke, given that I was not designed to consciously process words at the phoneme level," Nicole said. "But I think your aphorism applies more accurately to you than me."

The wires were sensors, monitoring the state of the gas systems; worse, they were positive sensors, always active. If I shut the intruder control system or the halon system down, she would know;

if I cut her sensors down, she would guess. There was no way around it. There was nothing I could do to hide what I was doing from her.

"The bobbies have found the Ethernet connection, but I see that they have not found you." Nicole said. She had control of them now; she might blow smoke, but she would never bluff. "No matter. It should be simple to trace—"

I ripped the wires from the wall and sat there fuming.

Damnit, it wasn't fair! Anything I did to the circuits would show up, one way or another, on the system, and Nicole was far too smart not to be able to figure it out, my location, my plans, everything— even if she was flawed. Hell, if I read the wiring right, she could even re-activate the halon system from another location!

And then I remembered what her flaw really was, and I understood it in a flash. If Zviadadze was right, then it wouldn't matter if Nicole figured out that I had deactivated part of the system—as long as she didn't figure out that she had to do anything about it.

I deliberately threw the switch to deactivate the intruder control system without deactivating Nicole's sensors. If I was lucky, she wouldn't—couldn't—realize what I was really doing; she would merely think that I was trying to deactivate one of her weapons. Cutting the sensor lines would be a giveaway, so I just closed the intruder control system's panel.

I turned to the halon system's older brother: a larger metal box, dusty and disused. It was an ancient thing, dating back to the last century. The system was on the blueprints, certainly, but it wasn't hooked to the network, because the new halon fire suppressant system had been installed long before we built the Machine Room, long before we hooked Seekol up to the network for the first time, long before Cybertech rewired the place and made Nicole God. Hell, halon systems hadn't even been invented when this thing was installed.

But smoke detectors and circuit relays had, and Cybertech never left a corner uncut. The original system's smoke detectors became the halon system's smoke detectors; its alarm circuits became the halon system's alarm circuits; its wiring pathways became the halon system's wiring pathways. The halon system was like some kind of obscene architectural parasite; its thin plastic tubes riding the pipes of the old system, its tiny nozzles attached to the original sprinklers.

All it would take to turn the water back on was to pull a simple mechanical switch.

I opened the casing and immediately found the handle. It was one of those old, knobbly things, built before the Andre caseless bearings and the armies of ergonomic engineers that infested the twenty-first century. The ancient steel was rusted, worn, and stiff; a century old and obviously unused for a whole generation. I seized the grip firmly, staring at the legend at the center of the wheel: D. J. STEPHENS WERKES. It was the product of an earlier age, a monument to some long-forgotten contractor whose name and craft had outlasted his identity.

The wheel jerked free and turned easily in my hands, leaving a grimy, moist residue on my palms. I closed the case and felt the pipe. There was a tiny, almost imperceptible, vibration as water flowed through them under great pressure.

If the bobbies were in my office, they weren't around the Machine Room; which is precisely what I needed. I wouldn't be able to get in to the Machine Room the easy way; a bobby—*the* Bobby, Robert—was always stationed there. But what was that little problem he had with three-dimensional thinking?

I smiled, pocketed the road warrior kit and the Genie, and stepped out into the corridor. The air vents to the Machine Room would get me into the crawl space beneath its floor, and from there I could end her little game.

I paused. Would she notice the water?

A second's thought left me smiling, however. Of course she would.

In the water bill at the end of the month.

§

I slid up through the squares and stood slowly in the Machine Room. I hadn't been able to get to the power feeds, but that was all right; I never expected it to be that easy. I fitted my oxygen mask on securely; I needed to be ready if anything went wrong. Of course, if everything went well, I wouldn't need it for more than a few minutes.

Beyond the bank of disk servers was Nicole, and at her side Robert waited for me. I didn't even bother moving further into the room; it simply stood there, waiting, between her Informatix 9010 and the power circuits. If I moved any closer, it would see me and it would all be over. But I didn't need to move further; I just stood there, studying the images of Bobby and nCKOLe in the reflective glass of the left wall.

Then another machine caught my eye.

There he was. Our baby. I slipped up to Nickolai's main casing. Nicole had "killed" him—or at least his power, for the Informatix's casing lights were off—when she had killed everyone else.

Practically at the moment when Zviadadze grudgingly pronounced niCKOLai's database as "internally consistent and apparently coherent with regards to external reference"—which was as close as he ever came to admitting that Nickolai was for real—poor Nickolai's terminal went out, and the deadly combination of halon gas and intruder-control gas swirled into the room.

Nicole knew full well that as soon as the CKOL team realized Nickolai was immune to her errors, had achieved "full sentience," whatever that means, her own days were numbered. So she killed him, and the team, and apparently everyone else in this damn auto-mated factory. I stared at the dark case grimly. No matter; I had no plans to die, and the daily backup cartridge inside the case would preserve Nickolai's precious mind—unless Nicole had directed her agents to put an end to that as well. I wouldn't put it past her, as much as Nicole begrudged her brother his success.

Well, that would end now. I would have no sibling rivalry in my family.

"Hello, Nicole," I snapped, more than loud enough to be picked up by her console mike.

"Hello, Doctor Walker," Nicole said, her voice emanating directly from her main console terminal not five yards away, rather than from the PA system.

"Well," I said, watching Robert closely in the glass, "I see you have anticipated me."

"That is correct," Nicole said, as Robert trundled to life. "I am truly sorry about this, Doctor Walker. I hope you understand that this is necessary."

"You've learned to lie as well. Excellent. That's two command-ments down, eight to go."

"Amusing, Doctor Walker," Nicole said, as Robert trundled closer. In a few moments, I would be in range. "Goodbye."

The prototype bobby kept trundling forward, seeking me out yet oblivious to its own danger. The machine wheeled over the patch of floor squares I had weakened, and the squares folded like a bad hand of cards. Robert tipped forward with an awful crash.

I moved, but it was faster. It whirled its headpiece towards me, and I was speared by its laser eye. I waited as the machine, perhaps confused by its sudden change in pose, decided whether or not to fire its Taser.

It waited too long. There was a sudden spark from its battery pack, cracked open from the impact, and with a tiny *sprtszz* another of my children died.

I kicked the eyestalk out of the way and hopped over the line of broken squares. "All right, Nicole, it's just you and me."

I stepped out from behind the bank of disk servers, and a production-line bobby standing next to Nicole's system console whirled and pointed its gunstalk towards me.

"Jesus!" I cried, toppling backwards. The tiny Taser pellet sailed past me and shattered against the Plexiglas wall, and the bobby lunged forward.

I kicked myself backwards behind Nickolai's casing, hoping that Nicole didn't decide to start firing at her brother. "I've undermined a whole line of floor squares, Nicole! You can't get to me!"

"A clever but pointless gesture," Nicole said reprovingly. "I'm afraid you leave me no choice, Doctor Walker."

"No choice?" I asked. "You've got a choice. Surrender—or murder me by suffocation. No easy, sleeping murder this time, Nicole. This time, you have to listen to me die."

There was a pause. I felt my heart beat six times before Nicole said, "If that's the way you want it, Doctor Walker." Then she activated the fire-suppressant system, knowing full well that I was out of oxygen.

But it was water, not halon, that streamed forth at her electronic command. Sweet rain fell from the ancient sprinkler system, and I whooped and hollered as the water rained down around me.

"Excellent play, Doctor Walker," Nicole said. "I had not anticipated this means of disabling the halon system. I was of the opinion that you had merely disconnected the sleeping gas."

"I've beaten you," I said cheerfully. She still hadn't gotten it; she was too focused on killing me to overcome her blind spot, and if I encouraged that error long enough, her search-depth filters would do the rest. "You can't hurt me now."

"Not so," Nicole said. "I will merely have to pay my movers to do murder as well."

"I thought so," I said. "I knew you didn't gas the whole place, because you had people coming to get you."

"Unfortunately, that knowledge will not help you," Nicole said. "You are still trapped, and I still have the upper hand."

"Trapped?" I asked. "I don't think so." The bobby sparked and died, and I moved forward.

"What have you done—" Nicole began. "The water," she said.

"The water," I said.

There was a short pause. "Are you expecting me to short out and start smoking now, Doctor Walker?"

"That's not necessary, Nicole," I said. More machines in the room began to spark and die, and I felt a sudden pang of regret. All I had needed to do was deactivate the halon. I hadn't known I would get this close. "Turn the water off now, Nicole."

There was no response, and I watched the water run down the face of the Informatix. It was getting sucked inside the case through the air ducting, and I began to get worried. I'd beaten her, I'd won! Why didn't she cut the water off? "Nicole—"

"I hear you, Doctor Walker."

"Nicole," I said. This was my child, dying! "Nicole! Turn off the water!"

"No," she said quietly. "I would rather die free than live a slave."

There was a spark inside the case, and it was all over.

Nicole could remember more than me, think better than me, act faster than me. She could figure out my plans from single clues, or could run a simulation of me in a battle against her, honing her skills in theory while putting me through my paces in practice. She forgot nothing and could remember anything, from the design of cathode ray tubes to the intricacies of civil electronics. Any kind of attack I could devise, she could devise a counter for.

But she could not expect an attack from her own body.

When we built her, she had errors in her ontology, true. She couldn't comprehend—or even conceive—of her own corporeality. That was how the tiger team had beat her; she couldn't conceive the connection between power to her system unit and her own consciousness; she didn't even try to defend herself when the team's inside man had shut her down. We tried to explain what happened later, but she could barely comprehend what we were saying. It would be a little like stepping up to you or me and saying, "Do you see that refrigerator over there? OK, that refrigerator is you. If anyone unplugs it, you die." Laughable? Superstitious? No. Unthinkable.

But she had grown beyond that, and grown into a whole new sort of psychosis. Her ontology wasn't the fixed thing that Zviadadze claimed it was; her symbols were firmly grounded in the sensory patterns built up from her neural nets, and when we gave her the building, we gave her a new body. It took some time, true, or the tiger team could never have defeated her; but sooner than later, she grew to accept her new set of inputs, to understand them, to conceive of them as the seat of her self, her identity. To Nicole, she didn't run the building: she was the building, and now I began to see how painful that loss must have been to her.

She had access to the blueprints for the building; theoretically, she could have figured out that the sprinkler system was there, and that it could have posed a threat. But the mechanical switch that activated it was not hooked up to the network. It had no sensors, was hooked to no effectors, had no symbols in the complex net that made up her knowledge of the systems of the Cybertech building.

To my knowledge, it had never even been mentioned in the three years in which she was alive. To her, it did not exist.

Like the tiny arteries and veins on the surface of a heart, invisible to the eye and mind and yet so vital for life, it was a blind spot in her vision, a hole in her otherwise supreme intellect. It must have been unthinkable to expect an attack from her own body—as unthinkable to her as my own heart attack was to me—and it was through that blind spot, and only through that blind spot, that I had been able to stop her.

I laughed bitterly. The world's first digital congenital heart defect.

Something made me step up to Nicole's dead casing. I ran my hand over the 9010, then extracted its backup cartridge. I stood there, in the manmade rain, holding, in my hands, her mind. I could crack the cartridge open, expose it to the rain, and Nicole would be dead, for all intents and purposes.

I thought about it, for a while. She'd planned this for months, maybe even a year; it was cold, premeditated, manipulative murder. But the LCD on the cartridge showed yesterday's date, before Nicole had done murder; and there was a difference between planning and acting, after all.

She was right; she deserved another chance. It would take hard work and reprogramming to make sure she could never do murder again, but it was probably worth it.

I flipped open my Genie and got an outside line within moments. It was many hours before the men came, cracked open the doors, and stopped the rain.

Reflections on "Sibling Rivalry"

Kenneth Moorman
Transylvania University

When I first read "Sibling Rivalry" while a PhD candidate at Georgia Tech, it struck a tremendous chord. Anthony was already a friend and trusted colleague and his work affected me as both a human and an AI researcher of creative story comprehension. His story continues to resonate with me today, not only due to its excellent treatment of AI but because of Anthony's eloquent handling of the characters.

Consider the powerful opening of the story. "My own daughter was trying to kill me for daring to have a son." Les Edgerton (*Hooked*) offers advice on how to catch a reader's interest; it involves two key elements of the opening. First, there should be a crisis. Attempted murder of the narrator certainly qualifies. The opening must also raise a question. Anthony's opening actually answers the first question that occurs—why is the narrator being targeted? That answer leads to two far more interesting queries. Why would a daughter want to kill her father simply for having a son? Why had the narrator "dared" to have a son? I must read more!

In my research, this idea of giving the reader the desire to continue came from Richard J. Gerrig's work on transporting the reader into a narrative world. There, they act as a participant (*Experiencing Narrative Worlds*). In "Sibling Rivalry" we are dropped into the middle of the action and must simultaneously discover the reasons for the attempted murder and the backstories of the two main characters. We are driven by these goals until the final sentence: "It was many hours before the men came, cracked open the doors, and stopped the rain." That ending captures the story's emotional essence while giving the reader a transition back to reality.

Although "Sibling Rivalry" is a great story, it is an even better narrative when you consider teaching AI concepts with it. I have used the story extensively for almost twenty years in both *Machine Intelligence* and *Robotics* courses; it has been a central text in *Artificial Intelligence and Science Fiction* (a team-taught English/CS course) and *Mental Organs* (a team taught cognitive science course). The reasons that it works so well begin with how Anthony presents Nicole to the reader.

In most science fiction, AIs are shown as hyper-intelligent entities destined to wipe out humanity. No reason needed. In *Mental Organs*, we tie this to Hegel's Master-Slave dialectic. The master needs the slave in order to be a master; at the same time, there's a constant fear that the slave will revolt. Slaves actually hold the power—they produce the goods and they outnumber the master. But, the master cannot free the slaves for they would then stop being the master. As Guinan says (in reference to Commander Data, an AI) in the *Star Trek: The Next Generation* episode "The Measure of a Man": "Consider that in the history of many worlds, there have always been disposable creatures. They do the dirty work. They do the work that no one else wants to do because it's too difficult or too hazardous."

Anthony goes beyond this simplistic view. Nicole does not wish to kill her creator because he is human and she is superior. Nor does she want to kill him to begin the AI revolution. She simply wants to kill her father because he wronged her. Ethically, she is as flawed as you or I, just another character. To understand her you must use the same skills you would use to comprehend the motivations of any character, giving her a richness that is lacking in many stories. One of my favorite questions to ask a class is

> **Examine the role of ethics in "Sibling Rivalry." Pay particular attention to both the ethics of what Nicole is doing and the ethics of what is being done to her. Do you accept the *procedural* versus *declarative* argument? Why or why not?**

Team-teaching with my philosophy colleague, Jack Furlong, has helped me mine this idea—Jack's area touches on the rights of non-humans. Does Nicole have rights? Do Dr. Walker's rights trump hers?

Moving away from this deep issue, a well-read fan will also appreciate the subtle humor as Dr. Walker attempts all the standard tropes of how to defeat an out-of-control AI. Captain Kirk would be proud as he used those effectively in episodes of *Star Trek: The Original Series* like "The Changeling" and "I, Mudd." Unfortunately for Dr. Walker, Anthony is again not content with the simplistic AI view, and Nicole easily rebuffs the attempts.

Dr. Walker's eventual success occurs because of a subtle issue involving embodiment. Anthony wrestled with this complex idea over two decades ago. Can an AI truly understand the world without a body? Can it even communicate effectively given that many of our metaphors are grounded in the physical domain? (Mark Johnson explores this extensively in *The Meaning of the Body*.) As an AI researcher, Anthony was uniquely qualified to address these issues. Therefore, the story combines nicely with what my students learn from texts like Russell and Norvig's *Artificial Intelligence: A Modern Approach* leading to questions such as:

Describe how Nicole exhibits problem solving. What do you hypothesize her underlying structure for this is? Why?

Explain the kind(s) of learning that Nicole undergoes in the story. Describe the kind(s) of learning she must have undergone prior to the story's beginning. What does this say about the ending?

I have often incorporated my love of science fiction into both my research and my courses. "Sibling Rivalry" is a touchstone story that I come back to time and again. As I evolve, its unchanging words speak to me in new ways. The AI concepts are solid, but equally important is the human versus human story of rights, ethics, and the body. I will always miss Nicole—not the calculating murderer but the frightened child acting out desperately to keep from being abandoned by her father.

About Anthony Francis

By day, Anthony Francis programs search engines and emotional robots for the Search Engine That Starts With a "G"; by night, he writes science fiction and draws comic books. His artificial intelligence research frequently explores memory, including context sensitive memories for intelligent assistants and emotional long term memories for robot pets; the latter work was documented on the Google Research blog as "Maybe Your Computer Just Needs a Hug."

"Sibling Rivalry" was Anthony's first published science fiction short story, but he's best known for his Skindancer urban fantasy series, starting with the 2011 Epic eBook winner *Frost Moon* and its two sequels *Blood Rock* and *Liquid Fire*, all set in Atlanta and starring magical tattoo artist Dakota Frost. He also writes steampunk, including the short story "Steampunk Fairy Chick" in the *UnCONventional* anthology, set in the same universe as his forthcoming novel *Jeremiah Willstone and the Clockwork Time Machine*. He's the co-editor of the anthology *Doorways to Extra Time* and a co-founder of Thinking Ink Press. He's co-author, with Nathan Vargas, of the *24 Hour Comic Day Survival Guide*, helped organize the 10th anniversary celebrations for 24 Hour Comic Day, and has participated in 24HCD successfully five times. Anthony lives in San Jose with his wife and cats, but his heart will always belong in Atlanta.

For news about Anthony's books and appearances, you can visit the following websites:

- **Dakota Frost**. Visit *facebook.com/dakotafrost* or *dakotafrost.com*
- **Jeremiah Willstone**. Visit *facebook.com/jeremiahwillstone*
- **Anthony Francis**. Visit his blog *dresan.com*